This book is dedicated
to my uncles, aunts,
cousins, nephews, nieces,
grandparents, parents,
brother, sister, wife and kids!

Oh, and yes, I actually do
have a real uncle Ivan.

BEN

I'VE AN UNCLE IVAN

by BEN SANDERS

Thames & Hudson

WELCOME
TO PIE
COUNTRY

I've an uncle Ivan,
who's drivin' a pie van.

Ivan has a niece named Kate,
who's only got one roller skate.

Kate's two brothers,
Mitch and Mike,
both prefer to
hitch and hike.

CINEMA↳

BUS
STOP

Mitch and Mike's
young cousin Cooper,
thinks he's super
on his scooter.

Cooper's skinny sister Winnie,
looks too tall to drive a Mini.

Winnie has an aunty Sam,

who's missed at least a dozen trams.

Sam's befuddled nephew Gus,
drives a double-decker bus.

Gus's gran is called Maxine,
she's bought a brand new limousine.

Maxine has a
grandson Buck,
whose gut
gets stuck
inside his truck.

Buck has a zany
grandpa Wayne,
who flies his bi-plane
in the rain.

Pie in the Sky

ASE

Wayne has a son-in-law called Michael,
who loves to ride his unicycle.

Michael has a fab niece Gab,
who likes to blab
in taxi cabs.

Gab has a manly
cousin Morse,
who's in the force
and rides a horse.

But wait...
Where's Kate?

She's running late
on her roller skate!

And she's just missed her uncle Ivan,
who's gone drivin' in his pie van.

Ben Sanders began his career as an illustrator at the age of twelve, when his drawings were used on stickers and other stationery. A decade or so later, he was still drawing, this time for an advertising agency. As an art director at McCann Worldwide, Ben worked with General Motors, Mobil and 7-Eleven, bringing their products to life for the small screen, print and outdoor campaigns. Since 2006, he has been working as a freelance illustrator, his work appearing regularly in various magazines and books and in a number of major advertising campaigns. Ben has won several illustration awards.

First published in Australia in 2013
by **Thames & Hudson Australia** Pty Ltd
11 Central Boulevard Portside Business Park
Port Melbourne Victoria 3207
ABN: 72 004 751 964

www.**thameshudson**.com.au

16 15 14   5 4 3 2

ISBN: 978 050050 036 1

National Library of Australia Cataloguing-in-Publication entry
   Sanders, Ben.
   I've an uncle Ivan / Ben Sanders.
   9780500500361 (hbk.)
   For pre-school age.
   Choice of transportation--Juvenile fiction.
A823.4

Editing: Nan McNab
Design: Ben Sanders at The Milk Agency Pty Ltd
Type set in McLaren. Copyright © 2012, Brian J. Bonislawsky
Printed and bound in China by 1010 Printing